PRAISE FOR
COCONUT AND CHARLES

"**Ellena Vollmer's book, *Coconut and Charles*, is a powerful example of when a child's imagination is supported and encouraged to grow.** Her story highlights the whimsy and excitement that lives in every day, just waiting for us! Ellena takes us on a year's worth of adventure through the eyes of her sweet dogs, with her childlike excitement jumping off the page with every tail wag and tongue lick. A wish granted with Make-A-Wish® is focused on the child and their family, but Ellena's wish is here to be shared with the world."

—Make-A-Wish Eastern North Carolina

Coconut and Charles
by Ellena Aislynn Vollmer

© Copyright 2023 Ellena Aislynn Vollmer
Illustrations by Haji P.

ISBN 978-1-64663-936-6

All rights reserved. No part of this publication may be reproduced, stored in a retrieval system, or transmitted in any form or by any means—electronic, mechanical, photocopy, recording, or any other—except for brief quotations in printed reviews, without the prior written permission of the author.

This is a work of fiction. The characters are both actual and fictitious. With the exception of verified historical events and persons, all incidents, descriptions, dialogue and opinions expressed are the products of the author's imagination and are not to be construed as real.

Published by

köehlerbooks™

3705 Shore Drive
Virginia Beach, VA 23455
800-435-4811
www.koehlerbooks.com

COCONUT
AND
CHARLES

ELLENA AISLYNN VOLLMER

Illustrations by Haji P.

VIRGINIA BEACH
CAPE CHARLES

This book is dedicated to Russell Vollmer.

"I am always here with you."
—Ellena

About the Author
Ellena Aislynn Vollmer

Ellena Aislynn Vollmer, a sixteen-year-old girl from North Carolina, was fascinated with books and writing. She was a natural nurturer and giver of nonjudgmental ears. After her diagnosis of terminal brain cancer, Ellena's dream of becoming an author came into being with the help of the Make-A-Wish Foundation and Koehler Books Publishing.

Coconut and Charles was written when Ellena was only eight years old. She wanted to help find a cure and help children with this aggressive cancer that took her life just seven weeks after her diagnosis. A portion of the funds from this book will go to the Ellena Vollmer Foundation.

Chapter 1
A Great Day

One day, Coconut and Charles had a bath.
They really enjoyed the bubbles.

Their owner, Brian, enjoyed it too.
It was almost time to go to bed and dream of
happy things. Sleepy time was here at last!
Time to get some rest.

Charles and Coconut had a long day today,
playing fetch and taking walks.
Oh! How fun!

"Breakfast is ready!" calls Brian as the two
friends rush downstairs for breakfast.
Coconut and Charles were very hungry.
They were grateful that Brian made delicious food!

Time for a **walk!**

Charles and Coconut are **well energized** and ready for Brian's **birthday**!

Lola made a **wonderful cake**!
She even made **doggy biscuits**
for Coconut and Charles!

Everybody **enjoyed the party**, especially Brian.

After the party, Coconut and Charles
played fetch for the rest of the day.
They had a **long day** as always;
it seemed to last **forever**!

Chapter 2
Pool Party

Yay!

It's time for Coconut and Charles
to set up the pool party with Brian!

They set up chairs, tables, food, plates, forks, knives, anything you could think of!

Oh, how fun this pool party will be!

Guests have started to arrive,
and their main interest is the pool
that Brian and the dogs set up.

Everybody is here!

Time to party!

Everybody has finished their **food**, and they are starting to **leave**. What a **great day!**

Brian, Coconut, and Charles all play fetch for the rest of the day!

Chapter 3
The Easter Celebration

How fun!
The day before Easter! Soooo much to think about.
Dog biscuits from Aunt Lola,
toys, bunny ears on your head. Wow!

"Good night, sleep tight, don't let the bed bugs
bite," says Brian. "Time for bed!"
(And I'm the narrator,
but I'm the one yawning most.)

As the dogs and Brian were sleeping,
the Easter Bunny came very quietly to give
Brian and Coconut and Charles
an Easter surprise!

Shhh!

"Morning, everybody!"
calls Brian as the dogs rush downstairs.

Coconut said, "If this is what the other bunnies do,
I'm going to start loving bunnies!"

Lola, James, and Luke arrived
with more Easter surprises!
They all, together for the rest of the day,
played fetch and ball.

Chapter 4
April Fool's

April Fool's Day is tomorrow. How fun!

On April Fool's Day, you do pranks and other cool stuff. Just think about it!

Dinnertime! Yay!
"Boy, oh boy, I was hungry!"
Coconut and Charles said together!

"Night night, Brian," Coconut and Charles said.

"Goodnight." Shhh!

"Breakfast is ready!" calls Brian.
Yum, yum!

"**Whoopee cushion** time!" both dogs say.
"**Ahh!**" screamed Brian.

More **pranks** continued that very day.

At the end of the day, Brian, Coconut, and Charles played **fetch** and **ball** with Luke, Lola, and James!

Chapter 5
The Haircut

Uh-oh, Brian's hair is **really long**!
"Ooh, I'm going to love my **haircut!**" said Brian.

Coconut and Charles loved Brian's haircut.
"Cool," said Brian. "Thank you!"

After Brian had his haircut,
they all ate lunch together.

At the end of the day,
they all played fetch and ball!

Chapter 6
They All Go to the Beach

Yum! Dinner! Coconut and Charles were hungry after their long day. Brian, too, had a long day. But now they weren't only energized but tired. They were all excited about going to the beach but also very tired.

Okay! At last, we can all say goodnight! Coconut, Charles, and Brian all went to sleep.

"Morning!" said Brian. "Yay, breakfast," said Coconut and Charles. "Yum!"

Okay, now that breakfast is over, it's time for . . .

THE BEACH!

"WOW! What a beach," said Coconut.
The beach was full of people with umbrellas.
The waves were huge, and there were sandcastles all over the place.
How fun!

"**Wait a second**. Is that what I think it is? A person is **drowning**!" Brian says.

Coconut, Charles, and Brian all **jumped in** and **saved him**!

WHEW!

"Thanks, dudes," the man said.
His name was Johan.

"We had no choice! We had to save you!"
they all said.
And from that day on,
Jonah was their best friend.

Acknowledgments

The family of Ellena Aislynn Vollmer would like to express our deepest appreciation to the following people. Without your dedication to this book, Ellena's dream would not have come true.

We'd like to thank Make-A-Wish Foundation, who stepped into our world and helped make a little girl's last wish come true. Emily da Camara and Karen Harris, you are doing God's work, and we are so very thankful for you.

To Haji P., your illustrations and art are like magic. You took Ellena's imagination and created these images as if you had pulled them right from her soul. We are so very thankful for you.

To Koehler Books Publishing, thank you so very much for the final product. Thank you also for your patience as we were mourning the loss of our beautiful daughter while putting this together. Her dreams came true because of you and your dedication. John Koehler—the mastermind and overseer—we appreciate all your direction and hard work. Danielle Koehler and Miranda Dillon, thank you for the countless emails and revisions and all your dedication to the book.

Russell Vollmer, we appreciate your gifts from the beginning, being by your sister's side and helping her. Every day and always. It has always been the two of you side by side. You helped Ellena realize her gift for writing, and you wanted to create books together. This is the first. She is always here with you, guiding you through this life. . . . You are never alone.

CPSIA information can be obtained
at www.ICGtesting.com
Printed in the USA
LVHW072008250223
740419LV00009B/396